DINO RANCH™

T-REX TROUBLE!

EPISODE ADAPTION BY **KIARA VALDEZ**

DINO RANCH and all related trademarks and characters © 2022 Boat Rocker Media.

All rights reserved. Published by Scholastic Inc., *Publishers since 1920.* SCHOLASTIC and associated logos are trademarks and/or registered trademarks of Scholastic Inc.

The publisher does not have any control over and does not assume any responsibility for author or third-party websites or their content.

No part of this publication may be reproduced, stored in a retrieval system, or transmitted in any form or by any means, electronic, mechanical, photocopying, recording, or otherwise, without written permission of the publisher. For information regarding permission, write to Scholastic Inc., Attention: Permissions Department, 557 Broadway, New York, NY 10012.

This book is a work of fiction. Names, characters, places, and incidents are either the product of the author's imagination or are used fictitiously, and any resemblance to actual persons, living or dead, business establishments, events, or locales is entirely coincidental.

ISBN 978-1-338-69222-8

10 9 8 7 6 5 4 3 2   22 23 24 25 26

Printed in the U.S.A.   40

First printing 2022

Book design by **Salena Mahina**

SCHOLASTIC INC.

It is a typical busy day at the Dino Ranch. Jon, Miguel, and Min excitedly race across the plain on an important Dino Ranch job.

No matter the hurry, the ranchers know that it is part of their job to take the time to answer any call for help.

Suddenly, they hear a loud cry from someone in need echoing throughout the plain.

"Whoa, Clover. Did you hear that?" Min asks as she slows down.

"Help us!" the cry rings out again. It is coming from just over the hill in front of them.

"Dino Ranchers, ride!" Jon yells. They take off toward the voice.

When they arrive, they see the Tinhorns had been the ones crying for help. It was all just a mean prank!

"Ha ha, we were just acting like we were hurt. And y'all fell for it!" Clara says.

"If you don't mind, we have work to do," Min says. "There is a wild Tyrannosaurus rex nearby that just laid eggs, and we need to make sure her nest is safe."

"Come on, Dino Ranchers. We have work to do," Jon says as he leads the ranchers away.

Once the Dino Ranchers are gone, the Tinhorns begin planning.

"If we got our hands on one of those eggs, we could have our very own T-rex," Clara says as they get on their raptors. "Let's ride, Tinhorns. We got us a T-rex egg to grab!"

After making sure the eggs are safe, the ranchers hear a loud cry from Ogie Tinhorn. "There's a big T-rex after Clara and Ike!" he yells.

But when they follow the voice, Ogie has disappeared! "I bet this is just another one of their tricks," Jon says.

While the ranchers are distracted, the Tinhorns are up to no good! They are getting ready to steal the tough, and very stinky, T-rex egg!

"Drop the egg!" Jon yells. A worried Min speaks up to remind him there is a baby T-rex in there! "But do it very gently!" Jon says.

"You Dino Ranchers are always so easy to fool," Clara says with a laugh.

Just then, the momma T-rex shows up with a roar! She is angry that someone has touched her precious eggs!

The Tinhorns dash off but not without tricking the Dino Ranchers yet again—they took the egg and left a rock behind! And now the momma T-rex is off to chase after the scent of her egg.

The Dino Ranchers must get to the Tinhorns and rescue the egg before the momma T-rex gets to them first! With the help of Clover's nose, the ranchers catch up to the Tinhorns in a narrow canyon.

After a big chase, the ranchers finally manage to
take the egg away from the Tinhorns.
"This egg belongs to its mother," Jon says as he
gently hands it over to Min.

And so the Dino Ranchers take off to return the egg to its nest, leaving the defeated Tinhorns in the canyon. All they wanted was their own T-rex.

Just then, the very angry momma T-rex shows up— she still thinks they have her egg! "But how can she tell the egg smell from our normal smell?" Ogie asks.

"She's a momma! And momma's nose always knows!" Clara explains. And the Tinhorns desperately begin yelling for help again.

The Tinhorns jump into a cave, but they are now trapped! Momma T-rex is waiting right outside of it. "Where are those Dino Ranchers?" Ogie yells, growing more scared with every passing second.

"They are not coming!" Clara whines. "They think we are pretending again!"

But the Dino Ranchers do come, because answering every call for help is more important than possibly being tricked. And they were right, the Tinhorns really are in trouble! Jon tries to talk to the momma T-rex but she continues to slam her head against the opening.

"It's not working . . . she just wants to go after the Tinhorns!" says a worried Miguel.

"No, she doesn't want them at all. She wants her egg back," Min explains, hopping off Clover.

"Over here!" Min shouts, quickly placing the egg in front of the momma T-rex. "You must be so worried. But your egg is safe and sound."

The T-rex slowly approaches the egg.

She sniffs it and then happily runs off with it.

"That was a close one!" Ogie points out. "Good thing you Dino Ranchers didn't mess up," says Ike. Even if they do not say it, the Tinhorns are grateful to have been saved.

Jon replies, "You're . . . welcome."
"No more playing tricks now, you hear?" Min says as she leads the ranchers home for dinner.

All in a day's work at the Dino Ranch. Even when they doubted themselves, the rancheroos stuck to their motto: Always answer a call for help!

PO# 5077903 04/22
Copyright © 2022 Boat Rocker Media
Scholastic Inc., 557 Broadway, New York, NY 10012